HIDDEN FROM VIEW

ANIMAL HIDEAWAYS

Written by
Anita Ganeri

Little
Simon

Illustrated by
Halli Verrinder

Little Simon

An imprint of Simon & Schuster Children's Publishing Division
1230 Avenue of the Americas, New York, New York 10020

A Marshall Edition
Conceived, edited, and designed by Marshall Editions
170 Piccadilly, London, England W1V 9DD

Copyright © 1996 by Marshall Editions Developments Ltd.

Editor: Jolika Feszt
Designer: Sandra Begnor
Consultant: Dr. Philip Whitfield
Editorial director: Cynthia O'Brien
Art director: Branka Surla

Printed in Italy
by Editoriale Libraria
1 3 5 7 9 10 8 6 4 2

Cataloging-in-Publication Data for this title is available from the Library of Congress.
ISBN 0-689-80265-X

Contents

Plovers

The ringed plover lives by the sea on sandy or pebbly beaches. The female does not build a nest. Instead she lays her eggs among the pebbles where the eggs' spotted shells hide them from hungry gulls. The mother's coloring also makes her difficult to see.

Plovers have long legs for wading through the shallows in search of food. They eat shellfish, insects, and worms.

4

If an enemy comes too close, the mother plover pretends to be injured to lead it away from her eggs. Then she flies off.

The plover usually lays four eggs. After they hatch, both parents care for the young.

5

Meerkats

Meerkats are small mammals, slightly bigger than squirrels. They live in large family groups, with 30 or more meerkats sharing a patch of ground. Their home is made up of tunnels and burrows below ground and feeding places above ground. Meerkats are fast, skillful burrowers and can dig hundreds of holes in a day.

A meerkat stands guard on a rock while two others dig burrows. Another meerkat is about to pounce on a scorpion

6

At the first sign of danger, the guard sounds the alarm and the meerkats dive into their burrows. Their main enemies are birds of prey, jackals, and foxes.

7

Octopuses

Octopuses hunt for food at night. By day they hide away in their dens in a coral reef. A den is hard to spot, with a tiny crack just big enough for an octopus to squeeze through. The female lays her eggs in the den, guarding them day and night until they hatch.

An octopus eats crabs. It creeps up on its prey, grabs the crab in a long tentacle, and kills it with a poisonous bite.

Crab

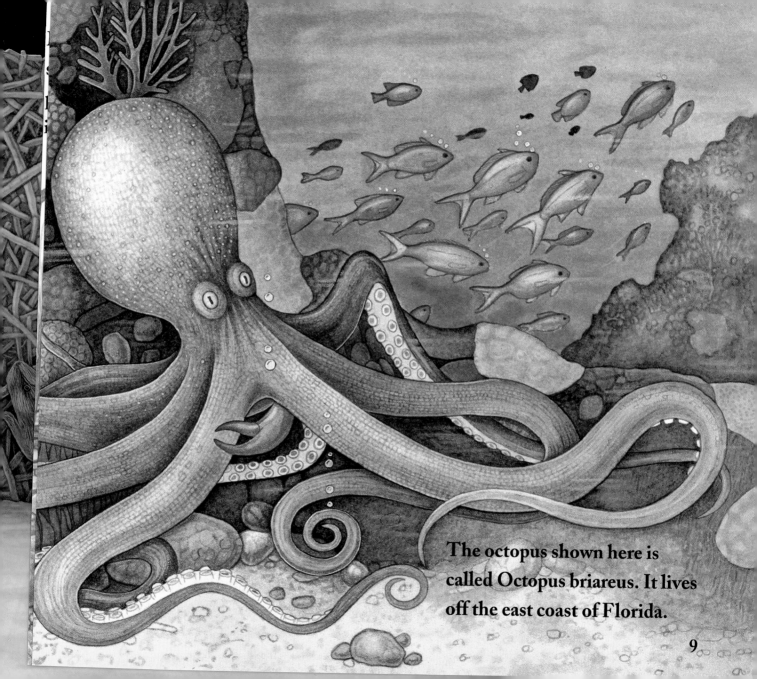

The octopus shown here is called Octopus briareus. It lives off the east coast of Florida.

Beavers

Beavers live in homes of wood and mud
called lodges. A beaver family constructs
a dam of sticks, stones, and mud across
a river or stream to form a deep pond.
The beavers then build a lodge
where they are safe from wolves
and other enemies.

The male stickleback makes a tunnel-shaped nest from waterweeds. Here, the female lays her eggs, as shown below.

Woodpeckers

A loud *tap, tap, tapping*
sound in a forest may be
a woodpecker pecking out a
hole in a tree trunk with its
sharp, strong beak. The hole is
used as a nest for raising young
birds. The female woodpecker
lays three to five glossy white
eggs in the nest. Then both
parents take turns looking after
them until the eggs hatch.
The bird shown here is called
a pileated woodpecker.

Woodpeckers love to eat ants, worms,
grubs, spiders, and berries.

16

Spider

Grubs

Ants

The eggs take three weeks to hatch. Little chicks are always hungry! Their parents are kept busy bringing them food.

Pileated woodpeckers live in the forests and woods of Canada and the United States.

17

Moles

Most of a mole's home lies underground. Piles of soil are pushed up to the surface as the mole digs a network of tunnels and burrows below. Because moles spend most of their lives hidden underground, they cannot see very well. They rely on their senses of touch and smell instead.

The piles of soil on the surface are called molehill[

Moles feed on earthworms that they dig out of the soil.

18

One of the burrows is lined with grass and leaves. Baby moles are born there in summer. They leave the nest when they are about five weeks old.

Honeybees

Honeybees are very sociable. Thousands of them may live together in a nest, which they often build inside hollow tree trunks. Here, bees make a honeycomb of six-sided chambers, called cells. Some cells are used to store honey. Others are used as nurseries for eggs and baby bees, called grubs.

The honeyguide bird from Africa eats bee grubs and beeswax. The bird gets its name from the way it guides people and other mammals to bees' nests.

Honeyguide

Most of the bees are worker bees They build the cells, keep them clean, and look after the grubs.

20

The cells inside the honeycomb are made of wax from the bees' bodies. The bees mix the wax with spit until it is soft enough to mold into shape.

The worker bees collect flower pollen and nectar to make into honey. Some of the honey is stored in the nest for when food is hard to find.

21

Polar bears

In winter it is freezing cold and icy in the Arctic where polar bears live. But polar bear cubs stay snug and warm in their den beneath the snow. In the spring they venture outside with their mother to explore and hunt for food.

The mother bear digs her den in autumn. She uses her huge paws as snow shovels.

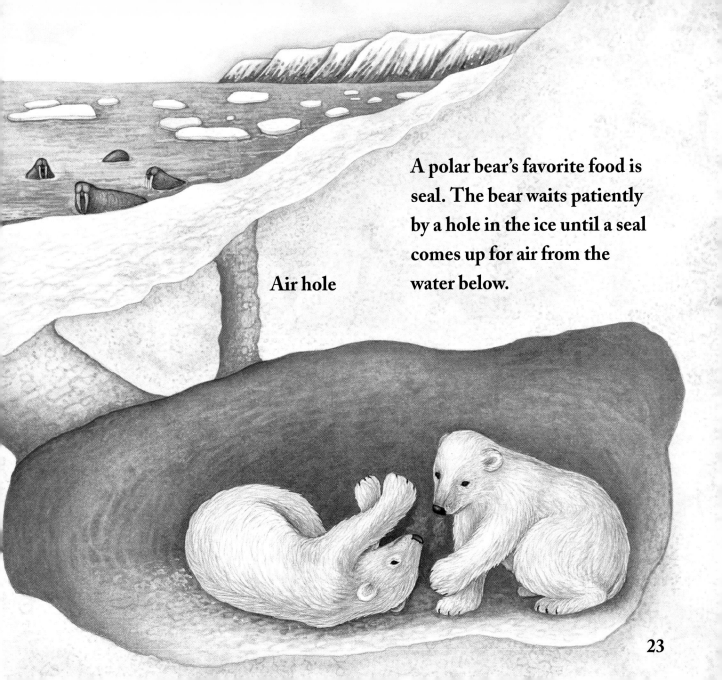

Air hole

A polar bear's favorite food is seal. The bear waits patiently by a hole in the ice until a seal comes up for air from the water below.

23

Index